THE FARM TEAM

For Maurice, with love and thanks — L.B.

For all the guys at Friday night shinny — B.S.

Kids Can Press acknowledges the financial support of the Government of Ontario, through the Ontario Media Development Corporation's Ontario Book Initiative; the Ontario Arts Council; the Canada Council for the Arts; and the Government of Canada, through the BPIDP, for our publishing activity.

Published in Canada by
Kids Can Press Ltd.
29 Birch Avenue
Toronto, ON M4V 1E2

Published in the U.S. by
Kids Can Press Ltd.
2250 Military Road
Tonawanda, NY 14150

www.kidscanpress.com

The artwork in this book was rendered in acrylics, on gessoed paper.
The text is set in Giovanni Book.

Edited by Debbie Rogosin
Designed by Julia Naimska
Printed and bound in China

This book is smyth sewn casebound.

CM 06 0 9 8 7 6 5 4 3 2 1

Library and Archives Canada Cataloguing in Publication

Bailey, Linda, 1948–
The farm team / written by Linda Bailey ; illustrated by Bill Slavin.

ISBN-13: 978-1-55337-850-1
ISBN-10: 1-55337-850-4

I. Slavin, Bill II. Title.

PS8553.A3644F37 2006   jC813'.54   C2005-907021-8

Kids Can Press is a *Corus*™ Entertainment company

THE FARM TEAM

Written by **Linda Bailey**

Illustrated by **Bill Slavin**

Kids Can Press

armer Stolski's farm was way up north where the ponds stay frozen most of the year. Winter lasts for ages there, and the farm animals might have grown tired of it — except for one thing.

Hockey!

Those animals *loved* hockey. The first snow barely had time to hit the ground before they were lacing up their skates. And oh, the excitement! Steam rose as the pigs passed the puck. Feathers flew as the ducks took shots. And when the goats hit the boards, you could hear them all the way to Winnipeg.

Every animal had the same dream. The Stolski Cup!

It had a rim of real gold! Many years before, it had belonged to Farmer Stolski's grandfather. He liked to sit by the pond and sip tea and snooze … until one nap time when the cup floated away.

That was the year the farm animals started to play hockey. They found the golden teacup frozen in the ice and dug it out. It became the prize for their first big game ever, against the Bush League Bandits.

The Farm Team lost that game. They lost every big game after it, too — for fifty years! But they never stopped trying. And they never stopped dreaming of bringing the Stolski Cup home.

So this year, they practiced harder than ever — even the animals who had no chance of playing. According to the rules, you had to be shorter than the net to play, so the cows were too big. The piglets were too small to be much use, especially the runt called Little Pete. And the chickens? Hopeless! They kept scoring on their own net.

But slowly, the team got better. They shot harder every day. And their goalie, a huge pig named George, was surprisingly fast. So on the morning of the big game, they felt a shred of real hope.

"Go, Big George!" yelled Little Pete. He watched proudly from the bench as his brother skated out.

Then Pete glanced across the pond, and his heart sank. Out roared the Bandits — the nastiest, smelliest, mangiest, snarlingest bunch of varmints you've ever seen. They had claws on their fangs and fangs on their claws, and even their *tails* looked mean.

The puck dropped. Seconds later, it was clear — the Bandits were going to play dirty. A porcupine named Needles started ramming Farm players. The weasels were slashing and spearing. And the goalie? What a skunk!

The Farm Team did their best. But at the end of the first period, the score was Bandits 3, Farm Team 1.

"We're such losers," clucked a chicken named Mariette, who sat molting on the Farm bench.

"No, we're not!" said Little Pete. "My brother George will hold them."

And for a while, he did.
As the second period began,
Big George blocked shot
after shot from the Bandits.

Then a goat named Billy
intercepted a pass and
scored for the Farm Team.
They were now only one
goal behind.

Suddenly, Needles charged the Farm Team net. He crashed —
full-speed — right into their goalie!

Big George went down with a horrible squeal. "Reeeeeeee!"
Dozens of quills stuck out of his padding.

"HEY!" squeaked Little Pete. "Needles did that on purpose!"

The porcupine got a penalty, but the damage was done. The Farm Team had lost their goalie. They huddled sadly on their bench.

Coach Clyde thought hard. Then he let out a neigh. "What about Betty?"

"Betty's a cow," said George. "She's too big to play."

"Maybe not," said the coach. "She's only a year old."

He galloped onto the ice with Betty. Sure enough, she fit — just barely — under the net.

"New goalie!" yelled Coach Clyde.

Now Betty wasn't fast, but she was solid, and when she stood sideways, she filled most of the net. By the end of the second period, she had blocked six shots. Meanwhile, a goose named Vera deked past the Bandits' goalie to score again for the Farm Team. The score was 3 all!

"See?" said Little Pete. "We can do it!"

"You think so?" said Mariette, peeking hopefully from under her wing.

At intermission, there was a flurry of activity on the Bandits' bench. A new player from the crowd was putting on a Bandits uniform.

Kreee! went the whistle to start the third period.

When the Farm Team saw the new Bandit, they started to shake.

"No fair!" squeaked Little Pete. "That's a GRIZZLY BEAR!"

"Sure it's fair," said the Bandits' coach. "He can fit under the net, just like your cow."

To prove it, the coach tried to stuff the big grizzly in. The bear didn't fit — not even close — but the referee was too scared to argue. He blew his whistle again.

Weak with fear, the Farm Team skittered onto the ice. One of the sheep had to be pushed.

"This is going to be baaaaaaaaad," he bleated.

It was awful! Little Pete gasped as he watched the bear smash, bash, whack, crack, slice, dice and fricassee one Farm player after another. The big grizzly was so mean, he terrified his own team.

"We're getting slaughtered!" cried Mariette as another player was carried to the Farm bench.

"We still have Betty," said Little Pete.

The cow had played her heart out. But she was trembling now and nearly on her knees. Little Pete looked around. Most of the Farm players were down.

Mariette was right. It was all over. They didn't stand a chance.

With two minutes left, Coach Clyde trotted down the bench.
"There's no one else," he said. "Little Pete, Mariette — you're in."
"Me?" squawked Mariette. "But I'm a chicken!"
"Chicken or not, we need you," said the coach.
Little Pete got bravely to his feet, and Mariette followed.
As they passed Big George, the goalie whispered in his little
brother's ear. "You're small. But you're fast. Go, Pete!"
The pig and the chicken skated slowly out to center ice.
Suddenly they stopped cold. Mariette's eyes widened in horror. The
puck came flying through the air … and landed right at her feet.
With a growl that shook nearby trees, the grizzly came at her.
"Pass!" yelled Little Pete. "Pass, pass!"

The panicky chicken whacked
the puck to the pig. Then she rose,
feathers flying, into the air. As the
bear raced past, she squawked and
dropped an egg — right on his nose.
The crowd roared with laughter!

Suddenly the bear swerved — to face the pig.

Little Pete froze. Then he remembered his brother's words: "You're fast!"

He tore off down the ice — straight for the grizzly.

The bear's paw rose like a hammer. His giant jaws opened.

"Faster!" thought Little Pete.

As the huge paw came down, he deked left! Then right! Then he charged between the bear's legs.

The grizzly wobbled, but just for a second. As Little Pete raced
for the Bandits' net, the bear was right behind — so close, Pete
could feel the hot breath on his back.

"Faster!" he thought. "FASTER!"

Putting on a burst of speed that shocked everyone, Pete
streaked ahead. He was practically flying!

He came at the goalie like a bolt of lightning. The goalie
leaped. Too late! Little Pete drove the puck right past him — into
the Bandits' net!

"HE SHOOTS! HE SCORES!" squealed Big George. "That's my
little brother."

The whistle blew. Game over!

The Farm Team had won!

"HIP, HIP, HOORAY!" shouted the crowd as Little Pete was hoisted high on his teammates' shoulders. "THREE CHEERS FOR THE FARM TEAM!"

Coach Clyde whinnied as Pete held up the golden prize. "HOORAY," he neighed, "FOR THE BRAVEST TEAM THAT EVER PASSED THE PUCK!"

And that's how, after fifty years, the Stolski Cup finally came home to the Stolski farm.

And the Farm Team is planning to keep it there!